DATE DUE

RON WEGEN
Sky Dragon

Greenwillow Books, New York

Library of Congress Cataloging in Publication Data

Wegen, Ronald.   Sky dragon.
Summary: The children look up at the snow-filled
clouds in the sky and see them as various animals
which give them an idea on what to build with the snow.
[1. Clouds—Fiction.   2. Snow—Fiction]   I. Title.
PZ7.W4233Sk   [E]   81-7219
ISBN 0-688-01144-6   AACR2
ISBN 0-688-01146-2 (lib. bdg.)

For Sean, Janis, and Althea

"My nose is cold."

"I see a dog."

"My hands are cold."

"Aren't those
elephants?"

"Yes, but my ears are going to fall off."

"What's happening?"

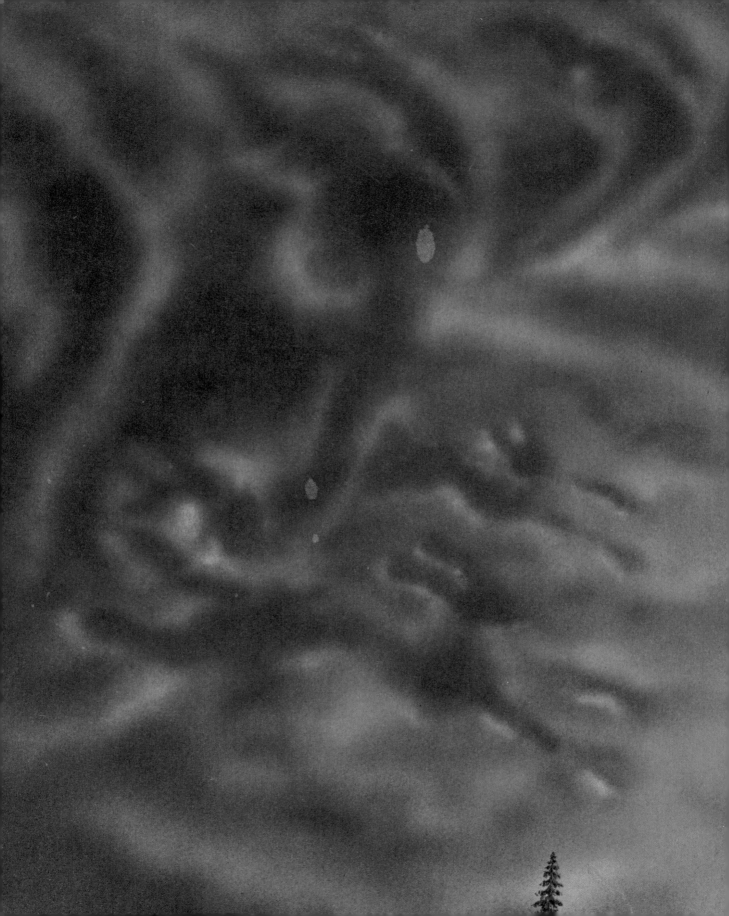

"*Wow!*"

"I want hot chocolate."

"It's getting dark. We better go home."

"It's
snowing."

"It snowed all night.
Let's build a snow fort."